MY GREAT-AUNT
ARIZONA

BY GLORIA HOUSTON

ILLUSTRATED BY SUSAN CONDIE LAMB

HarperCollins*Publishers*

MY GREAT-AUNT ARIZONA
Text copyright © 1992 by Gloria Houston
Illustrations copyright © 1992 by Susan Condie Lamb
Printed in the U.S.A. All rights reserved.

Library of Congress Cataloging-in-Publication Data
Houston, Gloria.
    My great-aunt Arizona / by Gloria Houston ; illustrated by Susan
Condie Lamb
        p.   cm.
    Summary: An Appalachian girl, Arizona Houston Hughes, grows up to
become a teacher who influences generations of schoolchildren.
    ISBN 0-06-022606-4. — ISBN 0-06-022607-2 (lib. bdg.)
ISBN 0-06-443374-9 (pbk.)
    1. Hughes, Arizona Houston, 1876–1969—Juvenile literature.
2. Teachers—Appalachian Region—Biography—Juvenile literature.
[1. Hughes, Arizona Houston, 1876–1969.   2. Teachers.]   I. Lamb,
Susan Condie, ill.   II. Title.
LA2317.H78H68   1992   90-44112
371.1'0092—dc20   CIP
[B]   AC

For all teachers,
members of the most influential
profession in the world
—G.H.

For Bernice Cooper Barrie,
with love
—S.C.L.

My great-aunt Arizona
was born in a log cabin
her papa built
in the meadow
on Henson Creek
in the Blue Ridge Mountains.
When she was born,
the mailman rode
across the bridge
on his big bay horse
with a letter.

The letter was from her brother,
Galen, who was in the cavalry,
far away in the West.
The letter said,
"If the baby is a girl,
please name her Arizona,
and she will be beautiful,
like this land."

Arizona was a very tall little girl.
She wore her long brown hair in braids.
She wore long full dresses,
and a pretty white apron.
She wore high-button shoes,
and many petticoats, too.
Arizona liked to grow flowers.

She liked to read,

And sing,

And square dance to the music
of the fiddler
on Saturday night.

Arizona had a little brother, Jim.
They played together on the farm.
In summer they went barefoot
and caught tadpoles in the creek.

In the fall
they climbed the mountains
searching for galax and ginseng roots.

In the winter they made snow cream
with sugar, snow, and sweet cream
from Mama's cows.
When spring came,
they helped Papa tap
the maple trees
and catch the sap in buckets.
Then they made maple syrup
and maple sugar to eat
like candy.

Arizona and her brother Jim
walked up the road
that wound by the creek
to the one-room school.
All the students
in all the grades
were there,
together
in one room.
All the students
read their lessons
aloud
at the same time.
They made
a great deal of noise,
so
the room was called
a blab school.

The students carried their lunches
in lard buckets made of tin.
They brought ham and biscuits.
Sometimes they had a fried apple pie.
They drank cool water
from the spring
at the bottom of the hill.
At recess they played games
like tag
and William Matrimmatoe.

When Arizona had read
all the books
at the one-room school,
she crossed the mountains
to the school
in another village,
a village called Wing.
It was so far away
that she rode her papa's mule.
Sometimes she rode the mule
through the snow.

When Arizona's mother died,
Arizona had to leave school
and stay home to care for Papa
and her brother Jim.
She still loved to read—
and dream
about the faraway places
she would visit one day.
So she read and she dreamed,
but she took care of Papa
and Jim.

Then one day
Papa brought home a new wife.
Arizona could go away to school,
where she could learn to be a teacher.
Aunt Suzie invited Arizona
to live at her house
and help with the chores.
Aunt Suzie made her work very hard.
But at night Arizona could study—
and dream of all the faraway places
she would visit one day.

Finally, Arizona returned
to her home on Henson Creek.
She was a teacher at last.

She taught in the one-room school
where she and Jim had sat.
She made new chalkboards
out of lumber from Papa's sawmill,
and covered them with black polish
made for stoves.
She still wore long full dresses
and a pretty white apron.
She wore high-button shoes
and many petticoats, too.
She grew flowers in every window.
She taught students about words
and numbers
and the faraway places
they would visit someday.
"Have you been there?"
the students asked.
"Only in my mind," she answered.
"But someday you will go."

Arizona married the carpenter
who helped build the new Riverside School
down where Henson Creek joins the river.
So Miss Arizona became Mrs. Hughes,
and for the rest of her days
she taught fourth-grade students
who called her "Miz Shoes."

And when her daughter was born,
Miz Shoes brought the baby to school,
to the sunny room
where flowers grew in every window.

Every year Arizona
had a Christmas tree
growing in a pot.
The girls and boys made
paper decorations
to brighten up the tree.
Then they planted their tree
at the edge of the school yard,
year after year,
until the entire playground
was lined with
living Christmas trees,
like soldiers guarding the room
where Arizona taught,
with her long gray braids
wound 'round her head,
with her long full dress,
and pretty white apron,
with her high-button shoes,
and many petticoats, too.

The boys and girls
who were students in her class
had boys and girls
who were students in her class.
And they had boys and girls
who were students in her class.

For fifty-seven years
my great-aunt Arizona
hugged her students.
She hugged them
when their work was good,
and she hugged them
when it was not.
She taught them words
and numbers,
and about the faraway places
they would visit someday.
"Have you been there?"
the students asked.
"Only in my mind,"
she answered.
"But someday you will go."

My great-aunt Arizona
taught my dad,
Jim's only son.
And she taught
my brother and me
in the fourth grade.
With her soft white braids
wound 'round her head,
she taught us about
the faraway places
we would visit someday.

My great-aunt Arizona died
on her ninety-third birthday.
But she goes with me
in my mind—
A very tall lady,
in a long full dress,
and a pretty white apron,
with her high-button shoes,
and her many petticoats, too.
She's always there,
in a sunny room
with many flowers
in every window,
and a hug for me every day.

Did she ever go
to the faraway places
she taught us about? No,
but my great-aunt Arizona
travels with me
and with those of us
whose lives she touched. . . .

She goes with us
in our minds.